Filomena's Friends

Book Two of "The Adventures of Filomena" Series

Fernando M. Reimers

Acknowledgements
I am grateful to the following friends who read a draft of this story and provided helpful suggestions: Sergio Cardenas and Mariam Cardenas, John and Linda Collins, Maria Paz Ferreres and Sofia and Tomas Marcilese, Saima Gowani and Zaahir Dadani, Ethan and Wilder Van Drunen, Armida Lizárraga and Isabel Bird Lizárraga, Lisa Lovett, Jennifer and Henry Norton, Catherine Snow and Juliet Baum-Snow, Ana Teresa del Toro, Pilar Velilla Arias, Matt Weber, Rose, Elise, Helen and Elliot Wettstein, and Noah Zeichner.

Illustrations and Layout: Tanya Yastrebova

Book Layout by Chrissy at Indie Publishing Group

ISBN-13: 978-0692173954 (Fernando Reimers)

ISBN-10: 0692173951

US Library of Congress Control Number: 2018909569

Create Space Independent Publishing Platform

North Charleston, South Carolina

This book is dedicated to Eleonora, my muse

Fernando

Chapter One. The garden

My name is Filomena and I live in a house on School Street, in a small town outside the city of Boston. Eleonora and Fernando live in the same house with me, they are my family.

I love the long days in the summer time. The colors are brighter, the sounds sharper. Everything around me just seems happier. On weekends Fernando takes me outside early in the morning. He comes to the living room and takes off the blanket that covers my cage at night and greets me: "Good morning Filomena. Did you sleep well? Do you want to come outside with me?" He takes my cage to the kitchen and puts it on the kitchen table. There he changes the water and food in my food dispensers, gives me a fresh leaf of lettuce, a twig of millet and a piece of fruit. He makes himself a cup of coffee and pours a glass of orange juice.

We then go outside to the backyard. He places my cage on a small table in the backyard, along with his cup of coffee and glass of orange juice. He brings the newspaper which he will read while he eats his breakfast. A big umbrella keeps us cool in the shade. The two of us just sit there and look at the garden. It is so beautiful. I look outside my cage and see the flowers: the hydrangeas, the rhododendrons, the viburnums, the azaleas and the roses. In the distance, I see the birdfeeder that hangs from a lamp post. Each morning Fernando will fill the feeder with sunflower seeds. Many different birds come to our backyard to have breakfast with us.

There are many different animals in our backyard. They are my friends. Can you see the bunnies hiding under the plants, and the squirrels running up and down the trees? Do you see the monarch butterflies and the bees, and the tiny chipmunks coming out of the holes they have dug in the garden?

This is Liberty the blue jay. Her feathers are blue like mine, and she has a long beak. She flies down from the tall maple trees that grow behind the fence. These are Charito and Luis, the cardinals. Charito's body is the color of an olive, she has an orange beak and a small crest. Luis is bright red, he also has a crest and an orange beak, and the feathers around his beak and neck are black, making it seem like he is wearing a mask. There are the sparrows: Gwang-Jo, Howard, Vikas, Felipe, Omolola, Rosie, Nell and Matt. Hummingbirds, doves and crows also visit our backyard.

Chapter Two. Liberty makes everyone mad

As soon as Fernando fills the birdfeeder with seeds many birds swoop down from the trees, as if they had been waiting for their breakfast. Liberty the blue jay comes first. She has the biggest body, and so she can't rest for long in the small perches of the birdfeeder. "Ooh so delicious and all for me!" says Liberty as she flaps her wings and scares all the other birds who are trying to eat. Liberty makes a mess as she gets some of the sunflower seeds from the birdfeeder, and many of the seeds fall on the grass. The sparrows go to the grass, where there are plenty of seeds for them to eat. The little black-capped chickadees, the purple finches, the American goldfinches and the rose-breasted grosbeaks fly around the feeder waiting for Liberty to leave, so they can take a turn at getting a few seeds.

Charito and Luis, the northern cardinals, don't like that Liberty is so selfish and when they approach the birdfeeder trying to grab a perch, Liberty scares them away. After Liberty has had her fill, she leaves and then all the other birds come and take turns on the perches, as they each grab a seed or two, and fly away. They each take turns getting food from the feeder. They know how to share the food, but Liberty does not seem to know how to share.

The branches in the Maple trees grow in all directions, some go over our yard, some over Mrs. Reuben's yard. They give shade to our garden and keep it cool in the hot summer days in Boston. As I look up at the trees I can see several nests. There is a big round nest which the squirrels have built. Three baby squirrels were born in that nest a few months ago, during the spring. Further up I see the nests of Liberty, the blue jay, where she lives with her family, and of Charito and Luis, the cardinals.

As Fernando reads the Saturday newspaper, I nibble on my leaf of romaine lettuce and talk to my friends who come to eat their breakfast. "Good morning, Fatima and Jack. How was the winter in Mexico?" I say to the Monarch butterflies who have only recently returned from their winter trip. "It was nice, Filomena" says Fatima. "We flew down with hundreds of friends from Massachusetts. Our small bodies cannot resist when it is too hot or too cold. This is why during the fall we travel to Mexico, where it is warmer, and in the summer, we come to New England, where it is cooler. We had a very pleasant time in the Michoacán mountains, staying in the Oyamel fir trees." "That is so nice Fatima, that you can travel such a long distance." "It is easier because we go with our friends, Filomena, many other monarch butterflies also travel the same distance. It is encouraging to do things with your friends, and we can travel such a long distance because we are not alone doing it, but have friends cheering for us and helping us."

"I agree, Fatima, friends can help us accomplish great things, and your long trip from Massachusetts to Mexico is a big accomplishment. My friends, the goldfinches and the rose-breasted grosbeaks, also travel to Mexico in the winter, as do the mallard ducks who have cousins in Mexico. I love my friends, and I know that they make our lives better. That is why I love to come to the garden to spend time with all of you. I find it so interesting to talk to you and learn about what you are doing."

As I am talking to Fatima, Sara, our next-door neighbor, comes over. "Good morning, Fernando—she says—and good morning Filomena. It's such a beautiful day, isn't it?" "Good morning Sara," says Fernando "May I offer you a cup of coffee?" "Sure, although I won't be staying long. I just came over to bring you a new plant for your garden. I know you love to garden," says Sara. "Well, thanks, Sara, this is a beautiful hydrangea indeed. I will plant it soon so that it goes on the ground as quickly as possible" says Fernando as he takes the pot with the hydrangea.

Chapter Three. Filomena has a word with Liberty.

Charito the cardinal comes over and says: "Good morning Filomena. What a beautiful day, isn't it? The flowers are in bloom and the sky is blue. If only Liberty made room for us to eat in the birdfeeder too." "Good morning Charito," I reply. "Let me talk to Liberty about sharing the birdfeeder." "Oh, I don't know, says Charito, she may not like it if you say anything. She can be quite a grouch, you know". "I disagree, Charito. This is what friends do, they stand up for each other, and they also tell each other what they need to hear. Besides, Liberty may not be aware that she is upsetting all of you. So how is she going to know if we don't tell her?"

"Good morning Liberty, can I have a word with you?" Liberty flies close to Filomena, and perches on one of the chairs around the table. "Good morning Filomena, it is good to see you."

"It is good to see you too, Liberty—I reply—I need to tell you something. You cannot be so impatient when you eat your breakfast and hog the entire birdfeeder for yourself while you eat. There are enough sunflower seeds for all of you, and you are making a mess and annoying Luis and Charito who are also trying to eat. I also see all the other little birds waiting a long time until you finish eating." "But I'm hungry in the morning, Filomena", she replies. "I know you are hungry, Liberty. We all want to have our breakfast. But you have to think about the other birds and share the birdfeeder." "That's easy for you to say, Filomena. That man feeds you alone in your cage and you don't ever have to share! I don't see why I need to share, I will have my fill first, because I am stronger, and the other birds can eat what is left when I have had my fill." I am sad to see that Liberty is so selfish, I wish I could help her understand she needs to share.

Chapter Four. The scare.

Liberty goes back to the birdfeeder and scares the sparrows away, who fly down to the ground foraging for Liberty's lost seeds. As Liberty is distracted eating as much as she can handle, she does not notice a hawk above the trees, slowly flying in circles. The hawk is hungry and hunting for prey. He has seen Liberty and is planning to have himself a nice little blue jay for lunch. He circles and circles looking to the best way to catch Liberty by surprise. I notice the hawk and realize what he is up to, so I shout 'Liberty, be careful, there is a hawk that is...'

I have not finished the sentence when the hawk 'suuuooooosh' flies down in an instant and grabs Liberty by a wing. When Liberty realizes the hawk is trying to pull her up, she hangs on tight to the perch with her claws and starts to yell: 'Somebody help me! Please help! The hawk is trying to take me away!' The hawk pulls and pulls, hurting Liberty who is barely hanging on to the perch on the feeder, and who is wearing down as she keeps yelling for help.

"Hello everyone, please go help Liberty. Don't let the hawk take her away!" I yell from my cage to all my friends.

The three squirrels hear my loud chirps and see what is going on from their tree and they race down to help Liberty. Charito and Luis also fly to Liberty's rescue, and so do the sparrows, and the butterflies. All of a sudden, all of them have surrounded the hawk as I give directions from my perch in my cage. "Charito, get on top of the hawk. Luis, pull him from his tail," I command. From my perch I feel like a conductor of an orchestra, with all my friends playing quite the concert around the hawk.

Even though my friends are each much smaller than the hawk, they are determined that he is not going to take Liberty away. The birds surround the hawk, pulling his feathers in all directions. The butterflies fly in front of the hawk's eyes. One of the squirrels hangs from the lamp post and whacks the hawk with her tail. Daphne the bumblebee comes and gives the hawk quite a sting. Disoriented the hawk lets go of Liberty and flies away from all these animals who have come to her rescue.

Liberty falls to the ground. She is exhausted and scared. I then call Fernando who has returned to the garden just at the end of the commotion and takes Liberty in his hand. "One of her legs is broken. The hawk pulled too hard as she was grabbing the perch. She will need to wear a bandage and a crutch until it mends," he says. "We did it! –I proclaim— we scared the hawk away from our garden and he did not take Liberty. I don't think he will be coming back any time soon. Thank you all very much for coming to Liberty's rescue and for working together".

Chapter 5. Liberty learns a lesson and apologizes.

The next day, after we have all recovered from the scare fighting the hawk, Liberty comes by my cage. "Good morning Filomena. I came to thank you for your help yesterday. I would have been that hawk's lunch had you not come to my rescue". She looks so meek with her banded leg and her crutch. "Good morning, Liberty—I reply—. I am sorry you were hurt by the hawk yesterday, but I am glad to see you are doing much better today. I was not the only one who helped you. I did it with my friends' help." "Yes, I know—says Liberty—that was quite something. I would not have expected such little birds and butterflies and bees and the squirrels to be able to scare such a big hawk away". "But Liberty, together we can all do much more than we can do alone and accomplish great things. Now if you don't mind, I would like to finish our conversation from yesterday about why we need to share." I come close to the edge of my cage as Liberty comes to the edge of the table. All the animals come around to listen to what I have to say. Andy, Bianca and Keith, the three squirrels who were trying to climb the pole of the lamppost, have stopped and are looking at me wide eyed. Fatima and Jack, the monarch butterflies, have come to rest on my cage. Daphne, Laurel and Soo Sheung, the bees, look at us standing on the leaves of the hydrangeas. Luis and Charito, the cardinals, are perched on the lamppost. Gwang-Jo, Howard, Vikas, Felipe, Omolola, Rosie, Nell and Matt have all come closer to my cage, and are perched on the chairs around the table.

"Let me explain why we need to share, Liberty" I say so they can all hear. "This garden is big enough for all of us to live happily. Each of us makes the garden better. When the bees eat the pollen from the flowers, they take bits of pollen from one flower to the next, and this helps them grow. Do you see the composter bin behind the pine tree?" "Yes, Filomena, the bin where Eleonora and Fernando bring all the fruit peels." "That's right, Liberty. There are many small insects who live in that composter and who turn all the leftover food into compost that can be used to feed the plants. These small insects help all these plants we enjoy and that feeds the bees." "If we can each help our friends live their lives, we make it possible for each to make the garden better. But if we only think about ourselves, it's easy to get in the way of others, and this will make them unhappy, and if they are unhappy the entire garden will be unhappy. You see, Liberty, we are all connected here, like one big family, and none of us can be really happy unless we help the rest of us be happy too. That hawk who tried to take you away yesterday, Liberty, he was only thinking about himself. He would have made all of us very sad if he had eaten you for lunch". "Oh yes, Filomena, that was quite a scare he gave me. I thought he was truly going to take me away" says Liberty. "But because all the other animals came to help you, Liberty, we scared the hawk away. Didn't we?" "Yes, you did, says Liberty softly. I am so grateful that you all helped me." "You see Liberty, when they came to your rescue, they were all thinking not just about themselves, but about you. They were looking out for you, because they are your friends." I reply as Liberty listens attentively.

"But Filomena, even if I try to think about the other animals in the garden," replies Liberty "There are so many of them, how can I remember what can make each one happy?"

"It's very simple, Liberty. Come here. Go to the edge of the window and look inside the living room. What do you see?"

Liberty the blue jay flies to the window sill and looks inside the living room.

"Tell me, Liberty, what do you see?"

"I see many things, Filomena. Mostly furniture. I see the stand where I know your cage goes in the evenings. I see three blue sofas, two rocking chairs, one piano, a small coffee table"

"On the wall, Liberty. What do you see on the wall? Right above the piano"

"I see a painting on a frame"

"What do you see on the painting?" I reply. I realize all the animals are still looking at me, their eyes turning from Liberty to me as we carry on our conversation.

"I see many people, Filomena. Children and grown-ups. They have different kinds of clothing."

DO UNTO OTHERS AS YOU WOULD HAVE THEM DO UNTO YOU

"That's right, Liberty. And at the bottom of the painting, in shiny gold letters, is the answer to your question. Fernando has read it to me many times. I know it is one of his favorite paintings. The letters say 'DO UNTO OTHERS AS YOU WOULD HAVE THEM DO UNTO YOU.'

"But what does that mean, Filomena?" replies Liberty.

"I think I know what that means" say Howard and Vikas, the sparrows, almost in unison.

"Thanks, Howard and Vikas, please explain it to Liberty." I say to Howard and Vikas who are standing next to me perched on a chair by the table.

Howard goes first: "Liberty, if you treat others the way you want to be treated they will know that you care about them, that you are been considerate", and then Vikas completes the explanation: "If we each treat each other that way we can each feel like we belong in one big garden, that we are one big family."

"I can see that," says Liberty "Thanks, Howard and Vikas for explaining what the painting means, and thank you also and to Charito, and Luis, and all of you, for coming to my rescue yesterday, when the hawk was trying to take me away, you showed me that you care about me. By being kind to me, you showed me I belong in this garden too, and that you respect and accept me. Your kindness is teaching me that you would like me to be kind to you too."

"That's right," says Vikas. "I would feel better if in the mornings, when we come to eat from the birdfeeder, we could all take turns, so I would not have to get to the grass to eat the sunflower seeds"

"I am sorry, Vikas," says Liberty "I did not realize I was hurting your feelings by not leaving room for you in the birdfeeder. I guess I was just thinking about myself, and forgot about you and all the others."

We are all smiling as we listen to the conversation between Liberty, Howard and Vikas. I think she has learned a lesson now. As we turn around we see three little baby squirrels come down their nest in the maple tree towards the birdfeeder to eat sunflower seeds. Liberty flies away close to them and says, "Welcome to our garden. There is plenty of food and space for you to eat and live. We will all look out for you, and we will especially keep an eye out for that hawk so he doesn't think he is going to have any of us for lunch. Even though he is much stronger than any of us, together we can scare him away. You just go and eat your food, just remember to leave some food for others, and to treat others the way you want to be treated" and as the three little baby squirrels bounce up and down under the birdfeeder, I munch on my lettuce leaf, enjoy our flowers and feel so grateful for all my friends and for our beautiful garden.

Questions about the book

What did you like most about this story?

What did you not like in this story?

Why does Filomena like the summer?

Who are Filomena's friends?

Where do Fatima and Jack travel each year on a long trip?

Why do they travel there?

What other animals travel to Mexico each year?

Fatima and Jack's long trip is made easier because they travel with friends. Can you think of something you do which is hard, but you are encouraged because you do it with friends?

Why are some of the animals in Filomena's garden not happy with Liberty?

What did Filomena do when she learned some of the birds were unhappy with Liberty?

What did Filomena tell Liberty about sharing?

Do you think Filomena made the right choice by speaking to Liberty? Why or why not? What else could Filomena had done?

If you were in Filomena's shoes and you saw that Liberty was taking all the food, what would you do? Why?

Have you been in a situation like Filomena's, seeing that someone is not treating others the way they would like to be treated? What was that situation like, and what did you do? Why?

How would you like your friends to treat you? Why?

How do you think you should treat your friends? Why?

What was the hawk trying to do when he came to the garden?

What did Liberty's friends do to help her when the hawk was trying to take her away?

What did Liberty learn from this?

What did Liberty do after she understood she was not been considerate?

Have you ever apologized to someone? Why? What was the result of your apology?

In real life, do birds and butterflies and squirrels communicate?

Is the fact that they can communicate in the story meant to be a metaphor?

Made in the USA
Lexington, KY
27 December 2018